The Eagle Who Thought He Was A Chicken

D1519451

JOHN L. SOLOMON

DEDICATION

This book is dedicated to my son Linwood. You are my Oney and you will always be an eagle.

ACKNOWLEDGEMENTS

First and foremost, I want to thank God for giving me the wisdom and understanding to give me the words to tell this story! He is the TRUE author and finisher of my Faith!

Thank you to my beautiful wife for standing strong through all she goes through and having the resiliency to bounce back. You are a jewel in my crown that keeps her head up and encourages me at all times.

Thanks to my mom Jessie Solomon the Queen of my heart. My late great father John Solomon sr. who gave me the keys to wisdom and impacted my life. My amazing sisters Joan and Jeanette Mann who mean the world to me. My brother Derrick a king who makes me proud in my heart every time I see him or hear of his accomplishments and his wife Phyllis and their children's milestones.

My son Linwood who shaped my fatherhood and contributed to a lot of my gray hairs. My lovely daughters, Daphene and DeLisha who are bright shinny diamonds. And my little princes Zoe who's love for me brightens my life.

My solid friends, David and Brenda Sowell who stood by me as friends and co-laborers in ministry through my trials and victories you were there cheering, frowning but always loving and supporting. Phillip Reid Sr., Mr. CEO, My Big brother who pushes me into my destiny every time we speak and share.

My brother Larry Wilson a country boy who does what he say he will do and loves Jesus, my ministerial partner.

My #1 cousin Valerie Banks , VV and personal trainer who helped me to drop all the weight and learn how to take care of this body.

To Lloyd "BJ" Bell and Annie "Boss Lady" Bell who opened the gates and put me in the Lion's Den, I appreciate the blessing of teaming up with you heavy hitters.

To my fans, associates, partners, and friends who opened their heart, lives, and souls to help me be an eagle!

Thank you!

TABLE OF CONTENTS

CHAPTER 1
IN THE NEST

Once upon a time there was a mother eagle by the name of Furdy. Furdy had three young sons; her eldest son, his name was Shaw, her second son, his name was Preta, and her third eaglet was named Oney. Shaw, being the eldest was very boastful and conceited but a proud young eagle. He felt indestructible and nothing could stop him. Next there was Preta who loved to rub his feathers, and admire his beak because he felt he was the most beautiful bird alive. Last and the least of the three was Oney. His brothers were large, strong, and handsome but Oney was small and frail in comparison to Shaw and Preta.

On a certain day when Furdy felt her sons were ready, "I want you to begin practicing spreading you wings in preparing to fly because mother will not be with you always and one day you're going to have to leave the nest", she explained to her eaglets. "Mother, I will be ready when that day comes, Shaw replied in his deep stormy voice, because I am so strong." Preta answered in his smooth casual voice, "Mother, is the world really ready for a good looking eagle like myself." Oney then whimpered out in his nervous and shaky voice, "I . . . I don't ever want to leave the nest...I don't ever want to leave the nest...I don't ever want to leave the nest!"

From that day forward Shaw and Preta would go out flying on Furdy's back and jump around the nest spreading their wings. They anticipated that big day when they would spread their wings and leave the nest. Oney would only tuck away in the nest and watch his brothers spread their wings.

He would watch in fear until finally Oney would just shake his head and cry. "I am never going to leave the nest and I will always be right here with mother", Oney exclaimed to himself!

CHAPTER 2
TIME TO FLY

On a cool morning Furdy arose very early and woke her sons up for a great day of flying. "Today is the day, she shouted! Shaw and Preta were so exited they couldn't control themselves as they both bellowed out a loud, "hip hip hooray!"

They were so excited because this was the day that they began their final flying test. Oney didn't say a word because he had not been spreading his wings and he was also afraid because he didn't know what to do. "It is time for you to leave the nest, Furdy explained, and I have something very important to share with you, but before I do, I must go get you some food for your busy day."

Shaw interrupted, "I'm ready to fly now mother." "I would like fat free fish before my flight mother",

Preta requested. Oney did not say a single word hoping his mother would change her mind. Furdy then stepped to the edge of the nest, she spread her large beautiful wings, and WOOSSH! She took off!

Shaw then declared, "this is a great day to leave this nest and enter into the world of eaglehood", in his deep raspy voice." Preta chimed in with his smooth tenor voice, "the time has come for the world to get their long awaited gift, me of course and I know the world has been waiting for me." Oney just closed his eyes, shook his head, and said in his nervous and frail voice, "I don't want to go; I don't want to go...l don't want to leave the nest!" As the young eagles waited while Furdy was out hunting for food, something horrible happened and she never returned.

In the meantime back at the nest, noon began to come around and Oney began to worry. "Where is mother, he asked, she's been gone since early this morning." She has never left us alone this long before he thought. Shaw and Preta just walked around the nest pacing and practicing their wing spread techniques wishing their mother would hurry back so that they could began their flight. "Where mother and what is taking her so long", Shaw and Preta questioned becoming impatient.

Evening time began to drift in and there was still no sign of Furdy. Nightfall approached and still Furdy had not returned. Oney did not get any rest and he stayed up the entire night looking over the nest wondering where his mother was.

CHAPTER 3

LEAVING THE NEST

As the warm glistening sun and the crisp mountain air introduced the new morning to Oney, he jumped from his doze looking for his mother. He had begun to think it was a dream that she had left and not returned only to find that she really was not there.

He managed to see through his tear filled eyes, his brothers looking into the clouds. Shaw looked at Preta and Oney then said, "Brothers, the time has come for us to do what mother has told us to do. She is not here, but she does expect us to leave the nest and enter eaglehood." So Shaw nodded his head towards his brothers, spread his large strong wings, as he had done many times, and with a loud WOOSSH; Shaw took off and disappeared into the sky.

Preta looked at Oney and declared, "My beauty cannot be contained by this nest and I must leave also, goodbye Oney." He spread his large, beautiful wings, as he had done many times and with a loud WOOSSH; Preta took off and disappeared into the clouds. "Oh my, oh my", cried Oney. "I'm all alone and there's no one here with me. I can't, I can't leave the nest, I can't even fly and I've never even opened my wings." "This is just terrible", Oney thought as he began to cry for his mother. He cried and he cried and he cried until he fell asleep.

Oney was awaken by a rumbling in his stomach. He had gotten very, very hungry and he looked around for food but there was no food in the nest. "I must leave this nest; I cannot stay here because if I stay here I'll starve to death so I have to leave the nest", Oney said to himself.

There was one problem and that was Oney could not fly. "I'm so afraid but I have to go", as he said summoning the courage to leave the nest. Oney then stood to his wobbly legs and talons attempting to spread his wings. "Ahhhh", he screamed out trying to force his wings open. He had trouble spreading his wings because he had never spread them before or even attempted to do it. "What do I do, I can't do it, it hurts too much", Oney said. After a little time had passed, Oney decided to stand up and try again.

"I must try again and not give up until I do it", Oney shouted. "Ahhhh, ahhhh, ahhhh", Oney screamed! Then all of a sudden with a loud, SHOOSH, his magnificent wings spread open. He was now happy and so excited that he had gotten his wings open that he was now ready to move to the next stage. "Now I must take off and fly but I don't know how", Oney said sorrowful. He looked up and became excited as the idea of what to do dawned upon him. "I'll just do like mother, he screeched, and just take off into the sky!"

"Whoa, whoa, whoa", he cried out as he stood on the edge of the nest looking down. He tried and tried to take off but he could not leave the nest and it dawned upon him that he could not fly. "What do I do now, I cannot fly", he said wearily.

Finally Oney figured it out. "I know what to do", he said as he hopped once again to the edge of the nest. Oney got to the edge of the nest and opened his wings as wide as he could open them. "I will just wait for a strong wind to come along and fly high off into the clouds." Oney waited and he waited and he waited and at last a strong gust of wind came by and with a loud WOOSH, Oney took off and he was gone!

The wind carried him away high into the clouds. "I'm flying, I'm flying, I'm flying", Oney screeched! Then all of a sudden the wind lifted from beneath his wings and Oney begin to plummet down. "I'm falling, I'm falling, I'm falling", Oney yelled uncontrollably! Then there was a sharp thud as Oney crashed into an open area of hard ground. Oney lay motionless in a lot of pain and when he tried to budge he discovered that he could not move his wings. As Oney lie on the ground, he looked up and he saw white images all around him before he passed out.

CHAPTER 4

IN THE CHICKEN YARD

Oney had no way of knowing that he had landed on a chicken farm. A young hen by the name of Samantha walked over to Oney as he lay on the ground unconscious. "He's so beautiful, he's so beautiful", Remy clucked. She then went and called all the hens in the yard to come and see this beautiful bird.

All the hens began to come around and admire Oney as he lie in the hen yard. "Oooh, ahhh", all the hens exclaimed with loud clucking as they stood around and marveled at this new creature on their farm. They had never seen an eagle so beautiful this close up before and lived to talk about it. All of a sudden coming through the hens pushing and shoving was a very rude and devious rooster. "Make a way, make a way, move out of the way", Mr. Bickerman snapped, "Move out of the way." Mr. Bickerman was a cunning rooster from Britain and the head rooster of the chicken farm. "Make way and let me see this thing", Mr. Bickerman said. "Wait a minute this is an eagle", he said to himself.

"Emergency meeting, all committee chickens report to the hall conference room for an emergency meeting at once", Mr. Bickerman ordered. All the committee chickens clucked and hurried to the hen hall conference room as they all clucked back and forth about the arrival of Oney. "Everyone settle down, now!" Bickerman screamed. "We have a very big problem, there's an eagle with two broken wings, lying unconsciously in the middle of my, I mean our chicken yard", he whispered in his sly British tone.

Then slammed his gravel on his podium, "what are we going to do about it?" One of the roosters said, "Bickerman he's hurt, we need to help him." Another one said, "He will eat us when he gets healthy, he'll eat us all, we have to get rid of him!" And then one of the other members said, "We can tell him he's a chicken like us, he is young and maybe he will not know the difference." They all laughed at this silly idea until Mr. Bickerman stopped laughing and all the others continued laughing. "That is ridiculous", screamed Mr. Bickerman as the others stopped laughing and began to agree with him. "I have a better idea, Mr. Bickerman explained, "We can tell him he's a chicken like us. He is young so maybe he will not know the difference and that way we can use him to protect us from the grey fox." They all began to clap their wings and say what a great idea Mr. Bickerman had come up with. As Bickerman and the chicken council made their way through the hens, Oney was regaining his consciousness. "Ahhh", Oney moaned in pain, "oh my wings hurt."

Mr. Bickerman then exclaimed in a fatherly voice, "My boy, my boy you had a nasty fall and we are going to take you to our hen hospital where you will be patched up and clucking in no time". "Huh, what do you mean clucking", Oney asked barely awake? "You will find out soon enough my boy, Mr. Bickerman whispered in his sly British tone, move him out and take him away." So the roosters and the hens grabbed him up and they moved him to the hen hospital.

CHAPTER 5

BECOMING A CHICKEN

Several weeks later Oney began to feel better and Mr. Bickerman walked in as Oney lay in the hen hospital looking around. "How are you my boy", Mr. Bickerman said to Oney. "I don't know, I don't know what's going on, I can't seem remember much", Oney replied, "All I know is that I was trying to fly and I..." Mr. Bickerman then interrupted, "my boy that was your first mistake trying to fly."

"You are a chicken and chickens don't fly", he said once again in his sly British tone, "sure we can jump up and flap a little bit, but we don't try to fly through the sky, are you crazy, you're a chicken!" Oney asked puzzled, "I am? How can I be a chicken when I don't look like you? "

Bickerman replied, "nonsense my boy, you are a full blooded chicken like the rest of us. You are just a little different and have to develop a little more but you are a chicken no doubt about that. What's your name anyway?" Oney replied, "I, I don't remember my name but I was never told I was a chicken."

"My boy, Mr. Bickerman began to explain, "all of us began in a nest and you began in a nest. All of us came out of an egg and you came out of an egg, just like us. So you are a chicken, my boy; a chicken just like us. I'll tell you what; your name is Clucker, the chicken. I like it and from now on you are Clucker. Come on say it with me."

"I am a Clucker?" Oney responded. "No, No, No", said Mr. Bickerman impatiently, say I'm Clucker!" Oney said weakly, "I am Clucker!" "Come on boy, say it with some emphasis, CLUCKER", Mr. Bickerman shouted! Then Oney with a loud screech yelled, "CLUCKER!"

"Good, very good', Mr. Bickerman exclaimed, "Now let me hear you cluck." Oney did not know what to do so he let out a loud, "clank!" Mr. Bickerman then said, "come on and cluck like a real chicken, cluck, cluck, cluck, you can do it." Oney once again let out a loud, "clank!" Mr. Bickerman now irritated said, "No, No, No, cluck not clank." So Oney tried with all his might to cluck but all he could do was clank. Mr. Bickerman then called for one of the young hens to come, "Remy ", he clucked, "See to it that this chicken learns how to cluck properly."

Remy came in and she was happy to have been called because she liked Oney and she knew he was not one of them. Oney took one look at her and he began to cluck and clank like no other chicken had clucked and clanked before because he liked her also. Remy practiced clucking with Oney and telling him about the hen yard for the rest of the day.

They practiced clucking together every day until soon Oney was completely healthy again and got up for the first time. The news went all around the hen houses and through the chicken yard about Oney's recovery. He is up, he is up, was the mantra of the day for all the chickens and roosters. Oney walked through the hen house and the chicken yard greeting everyone he met, "cluck, cluck, clank, good day and hello fellow chickens", Oney clucked. All the chickens were afraid and watched him suspiciously at first, but as time went on Oney begin to fit in and be accepted.

His wings were completely healed so Oney would walk around with his wings slightly spread. Mr. Bickerman instantly saw this as a problem and spoke to Oney once again with his sly British tone, "my boy why are you spreading your wings like that with your head held high?" Oney replied, "I don't know."

"You are a chicken", Mr. Bickerman explained, "and your wings are to be bent behind your back like this with your head down." Mr. Bickerman began to show Oney how to flattened his wings on his back and hold his head down. Oney lowered his head down and placed his large wings flattened against his back. "That's it my boy you have got it", Mr. Bickerman said. "Now let me teach you how to peck."

Mr. Bickerman begin to walk around poking his beak repeatedly into the ground showing Oney how to peck for corn and worms. "Ok, I think I can do it", Oney confirmed as he begin to strut like Mr. Bickerman and stick out his head pecking for corn and worms. "Good my boy, very good, very good, I think you are growing up to be a fine chicken", Mr. Bickerman said, "and added you are Clucker the chicken!"

Oney then said proudly, "I am Clucker and I am a chicken, cluck, cluck, clank." Bickerman and the chicken council had done it. They were proud of themselves as they all laughed and celebrated Mr. Bickerman for making an eagle think he was a chicken and act like a chicken.

CHAPTER 6
CHICKEN OR NOT

Oney had become a regular part of chicken farm life and everything went on as usual. Except for when the farmers would come out to get the eggs. Bickerman and the chicken council put together a system to protect Oney from being discovered by the farmers. Whenever a farmer would come out to the yard, all the hens would cluck loudly that the farmers are coming and immediately Oney would be rushed into the hen house where they would cover him up with hay to hide him from the farmers.

They told Oney he was a prized chicken and if found the farmers would ship him off to be sold or even stuffed. Now with their plan of hiding him from the farmers working perfectly and Oney thinking and acting like a chicken, they all lived happily together.

Until one day, Shady the grey fox saw something strange from the hilltop on the farm. "Hmmmm, that's an odd looking chicken", Shady said in his gruff voice, "let me take a closer look." So Shady eased closer and got behind a tree that stood close to the chicken yard. Attempting to keep his bushy tail undetected, Shady got real low and he crept up to the fence. Suddenly one of the roosters saw the grey fox and let out loud alarming, "cockle doddle doo, the grey fox, the grey fox is coming!"

Chaos and mayhem began to break out on the chicken yard. Hens and roosters were running everywhere as Shady leaped over the fence and into the chicken farm chasing and snapping at roosters and hens with his razor sharp teeth.

Oney was running around clucking and clanking not knowing what to do. He continued running around with all the other hens and roosters as they made their way into the hen house. Oney was the last one running for the door when boom! The door was slammed in his face. Once again Oney stood alone.

"Let me in, it's me Clucker", he clanked and shouted. Oney's cluck and clank that the chickens were so familiar with had now become a strange noise in the face of danger. Then all of a sudden he turned around terrified as he stared Shady, the grey fox in the face. He had not heard much about the dangerous grey fox but he was terrified seeing this type of creature for the first time.

Then Shady said in a low husky voice, "excuse me, my feathered friend, but what are you doing here on the chicken farm?" Oney found a little courage from within and said, "I am not afraid of you and I am not talking to you, and you are not going to harm me." Shady the fox answered, "Ok I understand, I think but I am Shady the fox and who are?" Oney said proudly, "I am Clucker the chicken." Shady the fox asked again in disbelief, "Who did you say you were?" Oney said again, "I am Clucker the chicken, Clucker the chicken!" The fox grinned a little and replied, "So you think you are a chicken."

Oney becoming upset answered, "Why are you laughing? I am a chicken, watch this." Oney then began to strut like a chicken and peck for corn and worms as he clucked and clanked. Shady looked on and he began to laugh at the display of Oney attempting to prove that he was a chicken.

As Oney clanked and clucked, Shady laughed and laughed. Shady began to laugh uncontrollably until he grabbed his stomach and laughed even harder. He fell over laughing and began to choke on his tongue. He then stopped breathing and he died with a huge grin on his face. Oney stood not knowing what to say or do when Mr. Bickerman peered out from behind the door of the hen house only to see Shady, the grey fox, laying on the ground not moving and Oney standing over him with his foot on his chest.

All the chickens came out and saw what looked to them like Clucker with his large talons dug in to Shady the fox. All the hens were so happy that Clucker has beaten their long time enemy the grey fox. Oney feeling very proud and accepted shouted, "I am Clucker the chicken, do not mess with Clucker the chicken!" They all were so excited that they threw a celebration for Oney, "hooray, cluck cluck, clank", they all shouted!

It was a great day on the chicken yard and everyone was happy, everyone except Mr. Bickerman. He did not like celebrations unless they were for him and he became troubled about Oney. He said to himself, "if Oney could kill the grey fox, what could he do to us." Mr. Bickerman became terrified and shuddered at the thought of Clucker putting his large talons around his slim body.

Immediately Mr. Bickerman called an emergency meeting of the chicken council early the next morning.

"We have a new problem on our hands", Mr. Bickerman said in his sly English tone. "It was good for Clucker the chicken to have killed our enemy the fox but we have been calling him Clucker the chicken for so long we have fooled ourselves into thinking that he is one of us. He is not one of us and he could Very well kill us just like he killed that grey fox. In case you all have not notice he has become quite larger than us." All the council shook their heads and clucked and crowed in agreement realizing the danger that they all could be in.

"I have a plan so listen closely, Mr. Bickerman began whispering to the council." He shared his plan with the council and all the council shared the plan with the chickens on the yard. Everyone was convinced of the grave danger that they were in and all agreed to Mr. Bickerman's plan.

CHAPTER 7

NO MORE CHICKEN

The day came when the farmers came out to feed the chickens, and the door slammed as it usually did. Normally one hen would cluck out and then all the others would cluck loudly to get Clucker to the hen house, but this particular time there was no cluck, not a peep, only Silence. Remy, who cared for and cherished Oney very much, knew of the plan to allow the farmers to see Oney clutching a chicken and she was very disturbed.

Now as the farmers came out and they saw Oney wrestling with young roosters play fighting as they always did. The farmers went back in and got their guns supposing Oney to be a hawk. As the farmers pointed their rifles at Oney, Remy in full distress let out a loud cry, "CLUCK, CLUCK, CLUCKER

LOOK OUT!" She clucked so loud that Oney leaped high into the sky just as a loud boom; boom sounded when the shots were fired that barely missed him. Oney begin to clank and run franticly as the farmers were shooting at him.

He glided over the fence just in time and ran into the forest. Oney was now confused and did not know what to do or think. He peaked at the chicken yard from the edge of the forest and saw the farmers standing in the field pointing in his direction. At that moment, Oney knew then that he could never return to the farm. Oney moved deeper into the woods not wanting to be captured by the angry farmers. He was so afraid and so miserable he just broke down and cried, "ahhh, what did I do, what is going on?" He sat under a tree and he fell asleep not understanding why he was familiar with the same feeling he was having.

CHAPTER 8

BECOMING AN EAGLE

Oney awaken to a big surprise the very next morning. He found himself perched high above the ground in one of the tallest trees in the forest. As he was trying to figure out how he got to the top of the tree, Oney heard a loud screech coming from above.

Oney looked up and saw a huge, massive bird coming toward him and landing on the branch beside him. The bird with his head up and his chest out looked directly at Oney. "Who are you", Oney asked. "The question is do you know who you are?" asked the large bird. "Well of course, I am Clucker the chicken," Oney said as proudly as he could, "that's right I am Clucker the chicken."

The large bird asked again, "You are who?" Oney said a second time, "I am Clucker the chicken."

The massive bird looked at him and said, "hmmm, so you think you are a chicken." Oney said, "Yes, I am", but not as certain as he did previously. The large bird replied, "If you are a chicken how did you manage to soar up into this tall tree?" Oney was puzzled at this already and said, "I don't know."

"If you think you are a chicken why do you have large talons as I do", again the massive bird quizzed Oney. Looking down at the talons of the bird and then looking at his own huge talons, Oney wondered but this time he did not say a word.

Then the massive bird seeing the look of bewilderment in Oney's face continued his quiz, "If you are a chicken why do you have such a long, sleek, and sharp beak like mine." Oney crossed his eyes and looked at his beak and wondered. The large bird now driving his point home asked, "If you are a chicken why do you have so many elegant and beautiful feathers like mine." For the first time Oney looked down at himself and saw all the beautiful feathers that were on his body and he was amazed. The large bird now had Oney's full attention and instructed, "Follow me; I want to show you something." The large fowl spread his wings with a loud SHOOSH followed by a WHOOSH as he took off from the branch.

Oney beheld the majestic bird soar off into the clouds and held his head down disappointed at not knowing now, who or what he was. The large bird looked back and saw Oney still on the branch and he swooped back around to land on the branch and said, "my friend, why are you still in the nest, why are you still standing on that branch." Oney replied, "I can't fly, chickens cannot rise like you just did." The large bird said, "Sure you can, just spread your wings and fly."

"Spread my wings", Oney repeated and at that moment he began to remember his mother how she use to tell him to spread his wings. Oney thought back to that time and he attempted to spread his wings. "Ahhh", he cried out in his attempt but nothing happened, "I cannot, I just cannot do it," he said. The large bird said, "of course you can, just like this", and SHOOSH his wings popped out in demonstration, long and beautiful.

"I'll try again", Oney said. He tried with all his might after having his wings laid on his back for so long it seemed as if they would not open and just as Oney was about to give up, SHOOSH, Oney's wings spread to an enormous size. Oney was so surprised as he looked at his wings he yelled in amazement, "My wings, my wings, they are so beautiful. Just look at my wings."

The large bird remarked, "That's right they are your beautiful wings, now let us go a step further and fly." The massive bird spread his wings and WHOOSH he left the branch as Oney watched him take to the sky. Oney with his wings spread said, "I can do it, I know I can!" The large bird flew back around and said, "You can do it Oney, believe in yourself. Oney thought for a moment why had the bird called him by that familiar sounding name and then he began again to focus on flying off the branch. "I AM FLYING, I AM FLYING, I AM REALLY FLYING", Oney shouted as he remembered the wind being beneath his wings as he flew through the sky for a brief moment before he had fallen. The large bird said. "Flap your wings Oney and soar!" Oney flapped his wings and began to mount up and soar above the clouds. "I am not just flying, why, I am soring", Oney screeched!

Oney was so excited, he began to do swirls and twirls as he soared through the air. He could feel the wind flowing through his as he recalled Mr. Bickerman telling him that chickens could not fly and in that moment he realized that he was not a chicken. The large bird motioned to Oney to follow him. While Oney followed, he began to slightly remember being in the nest with this large bird and that his mother was Furdy. Just as Oney was about to say something, the large bird guided Oney to a nearby pond of water. As they landed, the large bird seemed even larger as he moved toward Oney and motioned for him to step towards the water.

Oney then asked, "What did you call me while we were in the air?" "I called you Oney", said Shaw, "now look into the water." For the first time Oney saw a reflection of himself in the water. He then looked at the large bird in amazement, then looked at the water, and gasped, "hey you look like me, I mean you are in the water, we are in the water, I mean, I mean, I don't know what I mean!" the large bird began to explain, 'My name is Shaw", Oney was overwhelmed and interrupted shouting; "YOU'RE MY BROTHER! "That's right and you are nobody's chicken and your name is not Clucker, your name is Oney. You are an eagle not a chicken", Shaw bellowed out in his deep voice! Oney was shocked as Shaw told him who and what he really was. Shaw continued, "You are my brother and we are eagles, kings of the birds of the air, birds who ride on the wind and soar into the sun. We are far from being chickens!"

"Shaw, my brother, I remember now", Oney said joyfully as it all began to come back to him! "How is Preta and mother", Oney asked excitedly. Shaw replied, "Preta is fine and maybe one day you will see him again. I later found out that the day when mother left, some evil men captured her and broke her wing so that she could not fly anymore and that is why we never saw her again." Oney hung his head and began to become very sad and disappointed but mostly at himself.

Shaw then asked, "How did you ever believe you were a chicken?" Oney thought for a moment then he sadly and embarrassingly responded, "No one ever told me I was an eagle, mother never told me I was an eagle and the first time I was told what and who I was, they told I was a chicken and my name was Clucker." "Oney, no one is to blame except those who were afraid of you becoming your powerful and true self , but also, you never tried to spread your wings and see what you could do or be", Shaw answered.

"You are an eagle Oney, do not ever be anything less or let anyone make you feel less than what you are ever again. Mother is no longer with us but her spirit is alive in you because you survived. Now spread your wings and soar like the majestic and unique powerful creature you were meant to be!"

Shaw then spread his large wings and WHOOSH, he took off. Oney looked up and said, "you are leaving me, what do I do?" Shaw replied, "I must go now, I have to fulfill my purpose. There is greatness inside of you waiting to come out as you believe in yourself like I and mother believe in you!" Oney begin to be afraid, then he heard Shaw screech from above, "YOU ARE AN EAGLE, SPREAD YOUR WINGS, BELIEVE IN YOURSELF, AND SOAR INTO YOUR DESTINY!

CHAPTER 9

AN EAGLE ON HIS OWN

Oney found himself once again alone but this time he was not afraid. Oney took some time and looked admiringly at his wings, his beak, and then his sharp talons and he shook his feathers all over his now huge body. Looking into the water he said, "I am an eagle, I am an eagle and not a chicken." He then spread his wings, SWOOSH, and in one smooth swift motion he lifted off the ground, WHOOSH. He soared through the sky for days just enjoying the wind between his feathers and enjoying being an eagle.

Oney looked down below one day and saw the chicken farm and carefully landed on a fence pole near the hen house. "Clucker, Cl, Cl, Clucker you,

you, you, you are back, you are back we were so w,w,w,worried about you Clucker, we did not know what happened to you", Mr. Bickerman said lying and obviously afraid. Oney looked him directly into his chicken eyes and said, "I am not Clucker, I was never a chicken and I know what you tried to do to me! My name is Oney and I AM AN EAGLE, I am a beautiful bird, a king of birds and do you know what I could do to you with a squeeze from my huge sharp talons?"

Mr. Bickerman trembling and extremely terrified said, "No sir Clucker, I mean Oney, Mr. Oney please understand, oh I must go my head hurts", he now whimpered in a not so British tone that was never real. Mr. Bickerman quickly ran off as the thought of Oney breaking him in half filled his mind. It was later found out that Mr. Bickerman was not from Brittan but was hatched under a heat lamp in a laboratory and not really sure of who or what he really was. He was also kicked off of the chicken counsel and off the chicken yard. He was never seen again but believed to have been eaten by Shazzy the fox, Shady's sister.

Oney looked at Remy and smiled at her thinking how kind she was in trying to help him fit in. Then in one smooth motion, he spread his wings WOOSH, he took off. All the chickens stared up into the clouds as Oney disappeared out of sight. From that day forward is said that sometimes on the chicken farm, Oney could be heard flying over and letting out a loud screech saying, "I AM AN EAGLE, I AM AN EAGLE!"

The End

About the Author
JOHN L. SOLOMON JR.

A veteran of the United States Navy and received a Bachelor's in Education from Regent University and an Associate's degree in Religious Studies from Logos Christian College. He has served in ministry for 25 years. Apostle Solomon taught at East End Academy and in the Newport News Public School System most of his tenure was working with emotionally disturbed/ADD/ and ADHD students. He facilitated a mentoring and leadership program called, Perfect Gentlemen for male students who are college aspiring, considered at risk, single parent homes, and or with gang related situations.

In 2003 Apostle John Solomon founded and established Life Altering Ministries of Newport News, VA, an outreach ministry that empowered people to change their thinking, shed stereotypes, and transcend their boundaries.

He is also the host of a weekly Podcast on We Inspire Network blog talk radio called: "Strength from the Lion's Den. Apostle Solomon is married to the gorgeous Minister, Lady Lisa Solomon and he's the father of a son and three beautiful daughters.

STRENGTH FROM THE LION'S DEN

with host Apostle John L. Solomon, is a compelling talk show that discusses life's difficult situations and celebrates our great accomplishments through poignant issues, and empowering stories from a biblical perspective. It is a beacon of hope, a source of enthusiastic listening motivation, and fun. His relevant interviews entail an interesting array of thought leaders, ministers, celebrated personalities, and odds- defying difference makers. A program that brings the medicinal effects of humor, transcendent Godly wisdom, the efficacy of education, but primarily strength and hope to the weary and the overcomers from the source-hood of our connection with our Lord Jesus Christ. Apostle John L. Solomon applauds our unsung heroes and powers up broken men, women, who need strength, and encouragement. As someone who identifies with pain he will show you how to get up and stay up! Every Wednesday at 7pm on http://www.blogtalkradio.com/search?q=we+inspire +network+radio

Bring Me To Your Next Event!

If you need a speaker for a platform, a host for your forum, or a radio personality for your event,

explojohn@gmail.com

https://www.facebook.com/explojohn

https://twitter.com/ExplojohnJohn

757-602-9466

APOSTLE JOHN L. SOLOMON

Made in the USA
Monee, IL
04 October 2022